PROPERTY OF

DATE

"WE ARE SUCH STUFF AS DREAMS ARE MADE ON; AND OUR LITTLE LIFE IS ROUNDED WITH A SLEEP."

—*The Tempest*, act 4, scene 1

DATE

DATE

DATE

DATE

DATE

DATE

DATE

DATE

DATE

DATE

"Men at some time are masters of their fates.
The fault, dear Brutus, is not in our stars,
but in ourselves, that we are underlings."

—*JULIUS CAESAR*, ACT 1, SCENE 2

DATE

DATE

DATE

DATE

DATE

DATE

DATE

DATE

DATE

"ALL THE WORLD'S A STAGE,
AND ALL THE MEN AND
WOMEN MERELY PLAYERS."

—*As You Like It*, act 2, scene 7

DATE

DATE

DATE

DATE

DATE

DATE

DATE

DATE

DATE

DATE

DATE

"LIVE A LITTLE; COMFORT A LITTLE; CHEER THYSELF A LITTLE."

—*As You Like It*, act 2, scene 6

DATE

DATE

DATE

DATE

DATE

DATE

DATE

DATE

DATE

"Our doubts are traitors and make us lose the good we oft might win by fearing to attempt."

—*MEASURE FOR MEASURE*, ACT 1, SCENE 4

DATE

DATE

DATE

DATE

DATE

DATE

DATE

DATE

DATE

DATE

"GOOD COMPANY, GOOD WINE,
GOOD WELCOME
CAN MAKE GOOD PEOPLE."

—*Henry VIII*, act 1, scene 4

DATE

DATE

DATE

DATE

DATE

DATE

DATE

DATE

DATE

DATE

DATE

"*Have more than thou showest,*
speak less than thou knowest."

—*KING LEAR*, ACT 1, SCENE 4

DATE

DATE

DATE

DATE

DATE

DATE

DATE

DATE

DATE

"SELF-LOVE, MY LIEGE, IS NOT SO VILE A SIN, AS SELF-NEGLECTING."

—*Henry V*, act 2, scene 4

DATE

DATE

DATE

DATE

DATE

DATE

DATE

DATE

DATE

DATE

DATE

"LOVE ALL, TRUST A FEW,
DO WRONG TO NONE."

—*All's Well That Ends Well*, act 1, scene 1

DATE

DATE

DATE

DATE

DATE

DATE

DATE

DATE

DATE

"There is nothing either good or bad
that thinking makes it so."

—*HAMLET*, ACT 2, SCENE 2

DATE

DATE

DATE

DATE

DATE

DATE

DATE

DATE

DATE

DATE

"MAKE NOT YOUR THOUGHTS YOUR PRISONS."

—*Antony and Cleopatra*, act 5, scene 2

DATE

DATE

DATE

DATE

DATE

DATE

DATE

DATE

DATE

DATE

DATE

"The web of our life is of a mingled yarn, good and ill together."

—***ALL'S WELL THAT ENDS WELL***, ACT 4, SCENE 3

DATE

DATE

DATE

DATE

DATE

DATE

DATE

DATE

DATE

"WISELY AND SLOW;
THEY STUMBLE THAT RUN FAST."

—*Romeo and Juliet*, act 2, scene 3

DATE

DATE

DATE

DATE

DATE

DATE

DATE

DATE

DATE

DATE

DATE

"There are more things in heaven and earth, Horatio, than are dreamt of in your philosophy."

—*HAMLET*, ACT 1, SCENE 5

DATE

DATE

DATE

DATE

DATE

DATE

DATE

DATE

DATE

"AND THOUGH SHE BE BUT LITTLE, SHE IS FIERCE."

—*A Midsummer Night's Dream*, act 3, scene 2

DATE

DATE

DATE

DATE

DATE

DATE

DATE

DATE

DATE

DATE

DATE

"WE KNOW WHAT WE ARE, BUT KNOW NOT WHAT WE MAY BE."

—*Hamlet*, act 4, scene 5

DATE

DATE

DATE

DATE

DATE

DATE

DATE

DATE

DATE

"There is a tide in the affairs of men, which, taken at the flood, leads on to fortune."

—*JULIUS CAESAR*, ACT 4, SCENE 3

DATE

DATE

DATE

DATE

DATE

DATE

DATE

DATE

DATE

DATE

DATE

"IF I LOSE MINE HONOR,
I LOSE MYSELF."

—*Antony and Cleopatra,* act 3, scene 4

DATE

DATE

DATE

DATE

DATE

DATE

DATE

DATE

DATE

“A fool doth think he is wise, but the wise man knows himself to be a fool.”

—*AS YOU LIKE IT*, ACT 5, SCENE 1

DATE

DATE

DATE

DATE

INSIGHTS
an imprint of
INSIGHT EDITIONS

www.insighteditions.com
Tag us on Instagram! @insighteditions

MANUFACTURED IN TURKEY
10 9 8 7 6 5 4 3 2 1